Level F

WITHDRAWN

A Note to Parents and Caregivers:

*Read-it!* Readers are for children who are just starting on the amazing road to reading. These beautiful books support both the acquisition of reading skills and the love of books.

 The PURPLE LEVEL presents basic topics and objects using high frequency words and simple language patterns.

 The RED LEVEL presents familiar topics using common words and repeating sentence patterns.

 The BLUE LEVEL presents new ideas using a larger vocabulary and varied sentence structure.

 The YELLOW LEVEL presents more challenging ideas, a broad vocabulary, and wide variety in sentence structure.

 The GREEN LEVEL presents more complex ideas, an extended vocabulary range, and expanded language structures.

 The ORANGE LEVEL presents a wide range of ideas and concepts using challenging vocabulary and complex language structures.

When sharing a book with your child, read in short stretches, pausing often to talk about the pictures. Have your child turn the pages and point to the pictures and familiar words. And be sure to reread favorite stories or parts of stories.

There is no right or wrong way to share books with children. Find time to read with your child, and pass on the legacy of literacy.

Adria F. Klein, Ph.D.
Professor Emeritus
California State University
San Bernardino, California

Editor: Christianne Jones
Designer: Nathan Gassman
Page Production: Angela Kilmer
Creative Director: Keith Griffin
Editorial Director: Carol Jones
The illustrations in this book were created digitally.

Picture Window Books
5115 Excelsior Boulevard
Suite 232
Minneapolis, MN 55416
877-845-8392
www.picturewindowbooks.com

Printed in the United States of America.

**Library of Congress Cataloging-in-Publication Data**
Blackaby, Susan.
Riley flies a kite / by Susan Blackaby ; illustrated by Matthew Skeens.
p. cm. — (Read-it! readers)
Summary: After trying to fly his kite in different places, Riley finally finds the
perfect spot.
ISBN 1-4048-1586-4 (hardcover)
[1. Kites—Fiction.] I. Skeens, Matthew, ill. II. Title. III. Series.

PZ7.B5318Ril 2005
[E]—dc22                                        2005021450

# Riley
# Flies a Kite

EASY READER
BLA

## by Susan Blackaby
## illustrated by Matthew Skeens

Special thanks to our advisers for their expertise:

Adria F. Klein, Ph.D.
Professor Emeritus, California State University
San Bernardino, California

Susan Kesselring, M.A.
Literacy Educator
Rosemount–Apple Valley–Eagan (Minnesota) School District

PiCTUR
Minnea

Riley made a paper kite.

He painted yellow stars on
the front and back.

He tied on a brown string for the tail.
He added red bows.

Riley and his dad went out to
the backyard.

9

The wind did not blow.

The kite would not fly.

Riley and his dad took the kite
to the park.

13

The kite got stuck in a tree.

15

Where could Riley fly his kite?

17

He needed a place without
trees, and he needed a breeze.

19

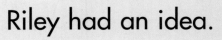

Riley had an idea.

He knew a great place to
fly his kite.

The football field at the school was the perfect place to fly his kite.

23

# More *Read-it!* Readers

Bright pictures and fun stories help you practice your reading skills. Look for more books at your level.

Looking for a specific title or level? A complete list of *Read-it!* Readers is available on our Web site:

**www.picturewindowbooks.com**